Phat Cat
Christmas Brat

Once upon a time, there was a Keynote named Phat Cat who was excited to celebrate her eighth birthday. Tomorrow, her family and friends would roll out a big birthday cake and tell her to make a wish.

But Phat Cat knew exactly what she wanted to wish for.

"I want to be Santa Claus!" Phat Cat shouted with glee.

"Are you sure you don't want to wish for something else, Phat Cat?" her friends asked. But she refused to change her mind. She wanted to be Santa Claus. She loved the story of "The Night Before Christmas," and she imagined traveling around the world giving presents to all the good cats.

The night before her birthday, her best friend, Tinka Cat, came over to her house and tried to make her see reason.

"Phat Cat, you're my best friend! I thought being Phat Cat was cool enough. You can write your own story," Tinka Cat said.

"But I want to be Santa Claus!" Phat Cat whined.

"You're being such a brat!" Tinka Cat yelled and huffed. "It's because you don't see how special you are! No one can perform like you. But Phat cat would not listen. I don't want to stay and play anymore," said Tinka Cat. And with that, she stormed out of Phat Cat's home.

That night was a very sad night for Phat Cat. As she hopped herself in bed, all she could think about was what Tinka Cat had said.

"I know I'm special, but I really want to be Santa Claus," Phat Cat mumbled to herself. "Is that so wrong?" But the more she thought about her wish, the more she realized that her best friend was right.

The next morning, Phat Cat plopped down on her
throne-like chair as her family and friends gathered
around and sang "Happy Birthday." It was time for
Phat Cat to make her birthday wish.

"Hold on, I want to say something," Phat Cat said.

Tinka Cat sighed with sadness, thinking that her best friend still wanted to be Santa Claus.

"My birthday wish is . . . to bring others gifts, and to have my own story told!" Phat Cat shouted.

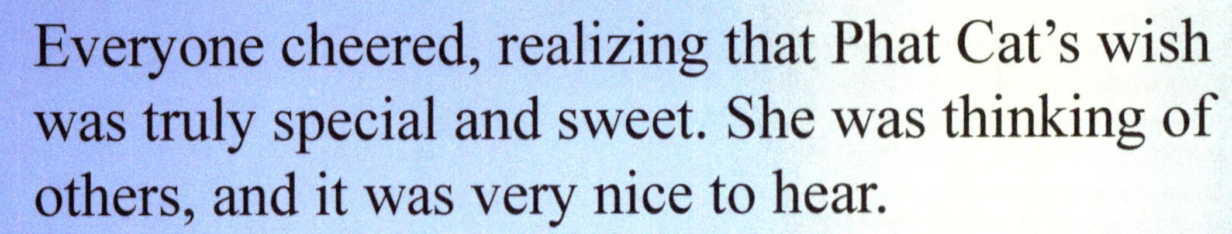

Everyone cheered, realizing that Phat Cat's wish
was truly special and sweet. She was thinking of
others, and it was very nice to hear.

"And yes, sometimes I'm a brat . . . but call me Phat Cat, please." Phat Cat winked at her family and friends. "I also have another gift for everyone!"

"What is it, Phat Cat?" Tinka Cat shouted with curiosity. Phat Cat wanted to do something for other people not just this birthday but every year on her birthday; after all, it was on Christmas Eve.

"I will deliver the gift of music to all the Keynotes…and to all the girls and boys…to all who need it and will use it." Phat Cat said.

Tinka Cat was so proud of her best friend; it was the sweetest thing she had ever done.

"I'm the Phat Cat Christmas brat!" She said with a snicker.

Later that night at the Christmas Eve party, Phat Cat told everyone a very unique story about her and her birthday wish. Everyone listened carefully, and everyone wanted to hear more. But the party couldn't really begin until Phat Cat performed.

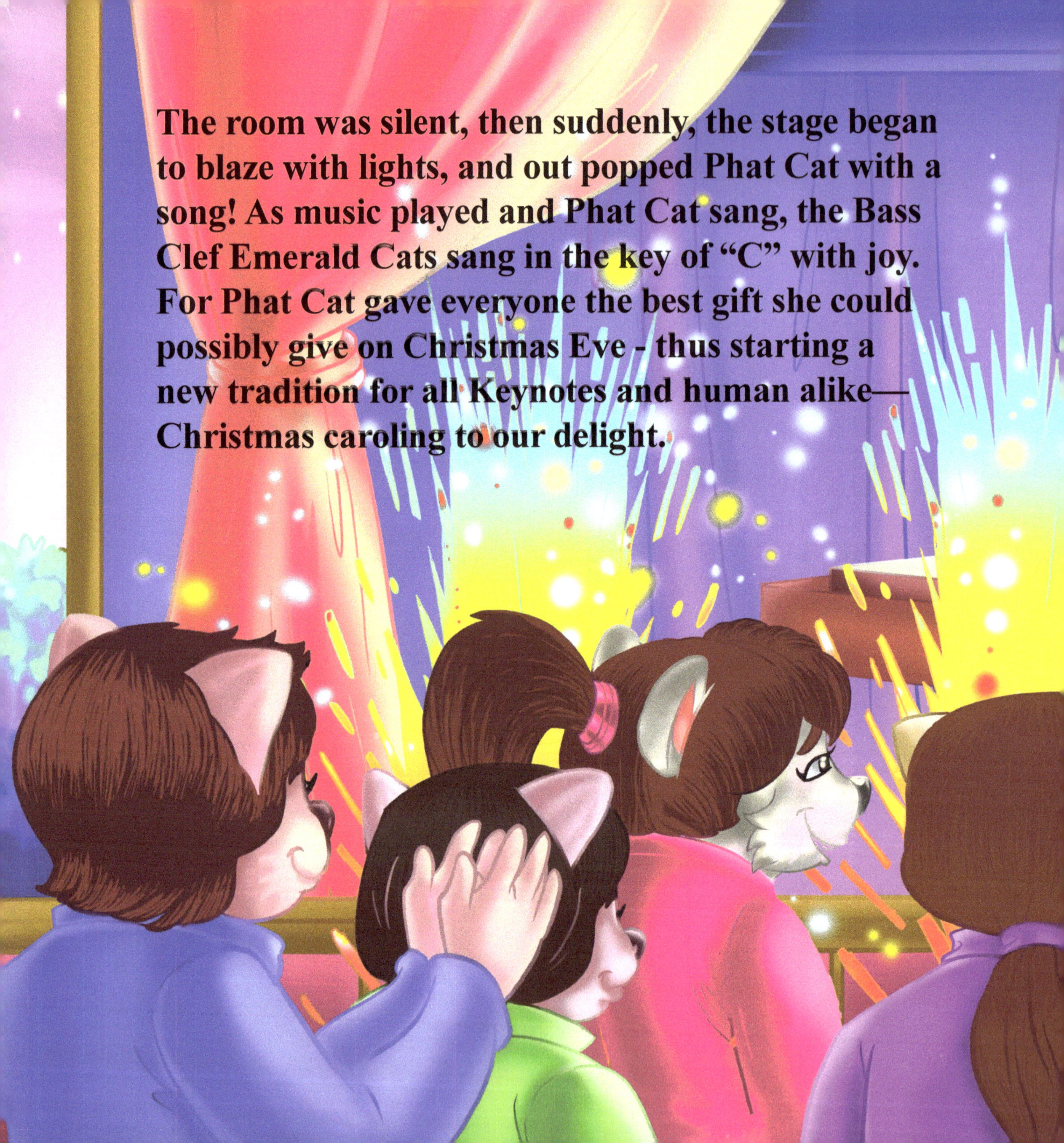

The room was silent, then suddenly, the stage began
to blaze with lights, and out popped Phat Cat with a
song! As music played and Phat Cat sang, the Bass
Clef Emerald Cats sang in the key of "C" with joy.
For Phat Cat gave everyone the best gift she could
possibly give on Christmas Eve - thus starting a
new tradition for all Keynotes and human alike—
Christmas caroling to our delight.

Check Out Our Other Titles:

Maps the Dog

Eli Emps

Izzy the Bear

Tiger Fairy Fish

Berry Berry Bear

Parkadian Pups

Merfish Race

www.ingramcontent.com/pod-product-compliance
Lightning Source LLC
Chambersburg PA
CBHW041202100726
47911CB00016B/831